The Waggiest Tails

For Judydog, who wrote many of the poems in this book, Jasper, who is yet to find his muse, and for Sam, who is not a dog.
R.S.

For everyone at Raystede Centre for Animal Welfare, Ringmer, East Sussex, and for my fox red golden labrador, Honey.
B.M.

For Rachel, Sammy, Flynn, Dixie, Daisy and Doodle
E.B.

Text copyright © Brian Moses and Roger Stevens 2018
Illustrations copyright © Ed Boxall 2018

The right of Brian Moses, Roger Stevens and Ed Boxall to be identified as the authors and illustrator of this work has been asserted by them in accordance with the Copyright, Designs and Patents Act, 1988 (United Kingdom).

First published in Great Britain and in the USA in 2018 by
Otter-Barry Books
Little Orchard, Burley Gate, Hereford, HR1 3QS

www.otterbarrybooks.com

A catalogue record for this book

ISBN 978-1-910959-89-3

Illustrated with a mixture of pen

Printed in the UK

1 3 5 7 9 8 6 4 2

The Waggiest Tails

Poems written by dogs,
with help from

Brian Moses &
Roger Stevens

Illustrated by
Ed Boxall

Otter-Barry BOOKS

Contents

A Book of Smells

Wouldn't it be good
if I could write a book
that dogs could read?

Not a book with words,
the kind of words that weave spells
through the reader's mind,
but instead
a book of smells.

Dogs could sniff their way
through my book,
as each new page
brings a different aroma,
each fresh smell
a new jolt to the nose.

From the dropped pizza
and brimming bins
of city alleyways
to countryside cows
and sheep.

The smell of rabbits
would get dogs leaping
from one page
to the next.

The smell of pies cooking
would get them
drooling.

To smell a rat
would get them racing.

Rich smells of perfumes
and caviar
would entice
celebrity dogs
from their cushions.

What a whole new dawn
for dogs,
what stimulation
from new sensations.

For Honey and Buster,
for Bumble and Nelson,
my book of smells
would quickly become
a best s(m)eller!

BM

Running with the Pack

There's me and Fido and Dido and Jack
Wolfie and Judy and Black
We arrive in the van with Uncle Stan
And he opens the back
And out we leap
And we're running and bouncing and barking
    and laughing
Running with the pack

Rolling in grass and catching the scents
And Wolfie's on the lead because he sometimes
    jumps the fence
Because there's interesting stuff in the field next door
But we're all free and we're chasing the ball
And Jack is a giant and Fido is small
And we're running with the pack
I'll race you there and back

And Dido wears a muzzle
He can be a little frisky
He'll nip you on the ankles, but it's only done in fun
And we bounce and we dance and we leap and
    we run
Because we're running with the pack
Yes, we're running and leaping and bounding
    and playing
Running with the pack

RS

Writing Poems

I find haiku too
sophisticated for my
doggy brain

But we dogs are quite adept at rhyming
Rhythm too, is our forté
So I'd rather write a pair of rhyming couplets
(or better still a pair of nice pork cutlets)
Any day

RS

The Old Devil

She calls me the old devil...

when I don't hear what she says,
when I'm having such hideous fun,
when I'm mapping a trail with my nose.
I just let the demon run.

It's that fabulous scent of freedom,
it's the chase over field after field,
it's the lure of a landscape that summons me
and nothing will force me to yield.

I can't calm the demon within me,
I just know it's taken control,
it's in my belly, it's in my legs,
it's in my heart and my soul.

There's nothing can stop me now,
I just let the demon run.
This old devil listens to nobody
till the chase is over and done.

BM

The Door Was Open

The door is open
and so I run out.
The air smells good
so I pause
for a good sniff
a little bit of poodle next door
and coffee from over the road
so I set off down the street
marking my favourite places
feeling good
without the lead on
and I pause for another sniff
and get traffic fumes and oil and
Cat!
and my nose zooms in
and it's over the road so
I race across
and cars hoot and screech
and there's a loud crash
but I have Cat in my reach
but then I hear my name
being shouted and it's Mistress and she says
Stay!

so I have to stop chasing Cat
and stay
and she says
Oh dear, and crosses the road
in between all the stopped cars
and crunches on the windscreen glass
and now I have to go back
with the lead on
and I can see Cat laughing at me
and Mistress is apologising to people
and I should have been quicker
and got away.

She's such a spoilsport.

RS

I Love to Chase

cows	courageously
squirrels	spectacularly
birds	creatively
rabbits	sneakily
pheasants	particularly
seagulls	wishfully
foxes	fitfully
bees	dangerously
frogs	occasionally
chickens	enthusiastically
sheep	rarely
herons	unsuccessfully

and

CATS of all kinds
wherever and whenever I can...

BM

What I Am

I'm a

human walker
cat stalker
biscuit snatcher
rabbit catcher (I wish)
tea towel fighter
dishcloth biter
insect hunter
deep sleep grunter
squirrel chaser
bicycle racer
sunshine dreamer
lazy schemer
noisy barker
nosey parker

of a dog.

BM

Call Me Yappy

I'd like to say, I don't sleep much
I like to stay alert
I'm not a nappy dog

And I like to keep my feet
firmly on the ground
I'm not a lappy dog

I never fight, or wrestle poodles
I'm not a scrappy dog

I don't play children's card games
I'm not a snappy dog

And you won't find me
down in the dumps
For I am a happy dog

But I get so excited so quickly
though I try to stay calm,
when my master says *Sit*
I have to admit I'm a yap yap yap yap
yap yap yap yap yap yap
yap yap yap yap yap yap
yap yap yap yap yap yap
yappy dog

RS

Walk Time?

I'm going to bark and bark and bark
or by the time we go walking
it will be dark.

But wait a minute…

He's fetching his coat,
it must be walk time.

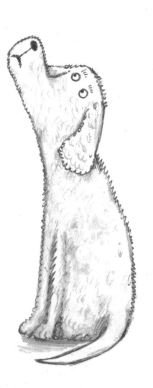

He's finding his shoes,
it must be walk time.

He's picking up his mobile,
it must be walk time.

He's fetching my lead,
it's got to be walk time.

But wait a minute,
his phone's ringing,
he's sitting down,
he's going blah blah blah.

And while he blah blah blahs
my walk's delayed

yet again.

BM

Don't Wanna

I don't wanna go to bed
don't wanna get up
don't wanna stop chewing
that smelly sock
I don't wanna stay
I don't wanna come
don't wanna stop chasing
the shadows in the sun
I don't wanna be quiet
I just wanna bark
don't wanna stop chasing
the ducks in the park
Don't wanna walk quietly
don't wanna walk to heel
and if you were a puppy
you'd know how I feel

RS

Bruno, the Smallest Dog

It's not so much fun being
the smallest dog on the farm,

when my short legs can't run
as fast as bigger dogs,

when my quiet little bark
doesn't scare anyone,

when the snow lies thick all around
and my tummy keeps bumping the ground.

But I do like being small
when I can run between the legs of labradors,

when I can squeeze through places
other dogs can't follow,

when I can steal from their food bowls
before they notice me,

when I can curl up between the big dogs' paws,
sleep between their feet and keep warm.

And I do like being small the best
when someone lifts me up

and finds that special place
for a vigorous tummy rub....

You should see the grin
on my face.

BM

Princess Zyara

I'm a Mexican dog, a regal chihuahua,
and my Aztec name is Princess Zyara.
We live in New York, my mistress and I,
in a penthouse apartment high in the sky.
I look from the windows and stare at the views
or play with her hundred pairs of shoes.
She feeds me on spoonfuls of caviar
and I feel just like a superstar
as I exercise each day indoors
so sidewalks won't feel the touch of my paws.

And if we should take a shopping trip
to somewhere downtown that's terribly hip,
I'm carried around in her designer bag,
an expensive dog with my own price tag.
All other dogs look with envy on me,
such oafish creatures, anyone can see
that I'm a chihuahua, so superior,
all other breeds are quite inferior.
I'm Princess Zyara, don't you forget,
certainly New York's most pampered pet.

BM

Gourmet

I am a gourmet dog
A fine dining dog
I eat only the best cuts of meat
Pheasant à la Mode is a firm favourite
Oysters go down a treat
I have an excellent nose
I drink only water from the best springs
Ah... here comes lunch
gobble
gobble
gobble
gobble
gobble
gobble
gobble
lick bowl
lick bowl
lick bowl

LOVELY!

RS

A Little Bit of This

I'm not a *bichon frise*
I'm not a *labradoodle*
I'm not a *moodle* or a *schnoodle*
I'm not a coiffured *poodle*
I'm a little bit of this
and a little bit of that
I'm a mongrel

I'm not a *pug* or *puggle*
or a *Belgian Malinois*
a *wolfhound* or a *whippet*
a *chow chow* or *chihuahua*
I'm a little bit of this
and a little bit of that
I'm a mongrel
Yes, I'm a little bit of this
and a little bit of that
and when all is said and done
I'm a bit of everyone
I'm quite pleased to be

a mongrel

RS

A New York Dog Shouldn't Have to Jog

A dog shouldn't have to jog
round Central Park on a Sunday.
A dog shouldn't have to run behind
his master's flying feet.
A dog needs time to sniff the air,
a dog needs time to stand and stare,
to meet and greet, to wonder how
other dogs are just allowed
to stroll and take the time they need.
A dog when free and off the lead
should follow his nose and not be tied
by invisible threads to his master's heels,
having no time to give dogs the eye.
With one brief look it's hello and goodbye,
be back again when our circuit's done.
No fun for a dog that has to jog
round Central Park on a Sunday.

BM

Paws on the Snow

We are huskies
we are ready and waiting
for there's no better feeling
in the midnight sun
than the jingling and the jangling
and the scent of the tundra
and the yelps and the growling
of everyone

There's ice in the air
and the sled is ready
and the humans are on board
and Togo's the one
who will lead us as we rush
like a wind through the tundra
through the crisp and the crunch
of the snow-blinding sun
and *Mush!* Off we go
and there's no better feeling
and the wilderness is calling
and the snow starts falling
and we are born to run

RS

Chasing the Hare

Eight of us
In our bright colours
We see the hare
And *whoosh!*
We're away
Round the track
The crowds cheer
And we catch the hare
Only to discover
That it's not real
It's never real
The race always ends in disappointment
The winner gets all the fuss
All we get is a biscuit
Then we all climb into the station wagon
And head home
To our cold kennels

RS

My Dancing Friends

I'm Charlie the Chihuahua
I dance the cha cha cha
And I'd like to introduce you
To my many dancing friends
First there's Fred, the friendly Foxhound,
    his foxtrot is quite hectic
Then Sam the Staffy, his Square Dance is exact
    and geometric
Pippadee the Poodle has a passion for the polka
Meg the Maltese Shih Tzu does a marvellous
    mazurka
Bob the Beagle breakdances, he's a fan of hip hop
Liz the Labradoodle has a Lindy Hop that's tip top
Tinkerbell the Terrier is tremendous at the tango
Her tarantella's terrific, and so is her fandango
Sun the Sussex Spaniel is a star at dancing zumba
And you'll applaud Zac Schnoodle and his
    scintillating samba

34

Shahrazad the Schnauzer likes to shimmy and
   to rhumba
Bill the Boxer dances ballet in a natty little number
Pam the Pointer's on her tiptoes, her Arabesque is
   like no other
Harriet the Harrier does the hitch-hike with
   her mother
Col the Collie leads the conga, Wes the Whippet is
   a waltzer
Marvin the massive Mastiff is a masterful moonwalker

I'm Charlie the Chihuahua
If you had to choose you'd pick me
My cha cha cha's so wonderful
One day I'll be on *Strictly*!

RS

Security Dogs

We're security dogs,
we're big bad bruisers.
Mess with us and
you'll be losers.

We patrol the yard
so you'd better listen,
we've jaws of steel
and teeth that glisten.

One look at us
and you'll be yellin'.
It's the scent of fear
that you'll be smellin'.

We're security dogs,
don't forget our names.
I'm Olive, she's Flo,
we're two tough dames.

Bet you won't admit
to anyone tonight
how two feisty females
gave you a fright.

How we chewed you up
and spat you out.
We're security dogs,
there ain't no doubt.

So if you ever climb
over the fence,
we'll take a bite out of
your confidence.

Ain't got no time
for no yakkety-yak,
we're primed and loaded,
out to attack.

BM

You're Not Coming In

Woof! Woof! Woof! Woof!
You're not coming in.
Bark! Bark! Bark! Bark!
You're not coming in.

Woof! Woof! Bark! Bark!
Go away! Go away!
Woof! Woof! Bark! Bark!
My mistress is away today.

And I don't care who you say you are.
And I don't care that you have a key.
And I don't care that you do repairs.
You're not getting past me.
What's that? You have a piece of meat.
That's bribery you know.
Hmmm… it's tasty. OK. Just this once.
I'll let you in…

Hello.

RS

'Doesn't Mix With Cats'

(Sign on the door of a dog pen)

I ain't no la-di-da dog
who cuddles up to a cat.
You won't find any cat space
upon my welcome mat.

Cats have been there for chasing
right down through history.
How any dog can make friends with them
is one huge mystery.

We've never made peace with cats,
it's always been out and out war.
Dogs have always fought cats,
it's always been tooth and claw.

A dog just needs his space,
not some in-your-face sort of cat
who climbs into bed beside him
or snuggles close on the mat.

Share with one cat today
and you'll share with others tomorrow.
It's dumb making peace with cats,
it can only bring you sorrow.

One minute you'll be relaxing,
stretched out, warming your paws,
then you'll hear the click of the cat flap
and in slinks the cat from next door.

So you growl and you snarl and you bark
and you do what all dogs should do.
But there really is no justice at all
when the one that gets thrown out is you!

BM

Hot Dog

Leave me where the pavement is wet,
I've walked far enough anyway.
I just want to flop down and forget
we ever left the house today.

It was shady in our yard,
the sun wasn't bothering me.
But walking has been really hard
as the temperature reached thirty-three.

There's water here I can lie in,
one wet spot in this heatwave town.
Beneath the hair, it's reaching my skin,
I can feel it cooling me down.

You can push and shove me around
but I'm a mountain that will not move.
I'm staying here pinned to the ground,
though I know you don't approve.

So leave me here, move on,
pretend I've been overlooked.
I just can't go with the flow
when I'm lying here feeling half-cooked.

But I know there's a dirty trick you'll play,
one that gets me up on my feet.
I just can't resist when I hear you say,
'Here's a treat, boy, something to eat.'

BM

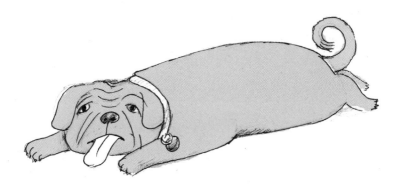

They'd Never Get Rid of Me...

They'd never get rid of me, I'm sure,
no matter how annoyed they get.

Not even when I disappear for days
in a field of wheat,
while they watch the crops wiggle like a wave
as I pass through.

Not even when I roll in something smelly
and they drag me back for a bath.

Not even when I'm wet
and my body becomes a huge shake
with water flying everywhere.

Not even when I go my own way
and wear my 'nothing to do with you' expression.

Not even when I terrorise next door's cat,
or shed enough fur to stuff a cushion,
all over the mat.

They'd never get rid of me
but, if they did…

they'd soon want me back!

BM

All I Do

It's all I do,
just hang around,
with my hang-dog expression
and my nose to the ground.

It's all I do,
just sit and wait
for the noise of a car
or the click of a gate.

It's what I do
and I do it well.
I wait for your voice,
your words, your smell.

Till I hear your key
and an opening door,
then I'm racing towards you,
scrabbling my paws.

Woofs and wags
are what I do best,
I wriggle about,
I leap at your chest.

I've perfected my own
crazy dog syndrome
to show you how happy
I am now you're home.

BM

Special People

I love the funny woolly ones
with the metal-rimmed eyes and white-top hair
who make those *ookylooky whattaprettygirly* noises
and stroke me and tickle me
behind my ear
I'm not so keen
on the little ones who start off
ooh, looky, isn't she cute
and then suddenly jump up
and go
Wahay! Bang! and *Crash!*
for no apparent reason
But my favourites
are the big ones
with the stick-throws
and ball-chuckers
and car-boots who say
let's go to the bigfield
and runthroughsome
mudandgrass

The havesomefun ones

RS

Just Watch It...

Just watch it or I'll come after you,
I'll sort you out in a flash.
I'll make you move so fast
you'll win a medal in the half-mile dash.

Just watch it now, I'm coming,
I've grabbed many children before.
I'll knock you down and nose you around,
then leave you flat on the floor.

I just like to show you who's boss,
but worse, far worse than this,
is when I pin you down on the ground
and give you a slobbery kiss.

BM

A Dog's Favourite Words

I have words
I understand.

Brilliant words like
barking
ball and **biscuit**.

Irritating words like
cat
and particularly
squirrel.

Adorable words like
dinner
and
treat.

And wondrously, whizzingly
wicked words like

WALKIES!

BM

WALKIES!

Bomb Detection Dog

(A dog's sense of smell is many times more powerful than ours and some dogs are trained by their handlers to sniff out hidden explosives.)

"Departure lounge." I hear his concern
when the call to action comes.
And we move in fast when he says, "Charlie,
it could be another one."

And the lounge is emptied of people,
silenced, as if holding its breath.
And the scent in the air that beckons me
may well be the odour of death.

But it's still my idea of a good time,
working from case to case,
watched over by my handler,
an encouraging look on his face.

 I've got a nose for what I do,
and I do it well, I know.
It's just like finding a stick or a ball,
I like being star of the show.

 I've no idea what's hidden
but my nose seems to sniff it out.
Then I sit down beside the case
as I hear my handler shout.

And at last my reward, the praise,
the pat, the biscuits I work for.
And I sense the relief in the air
as I'm led back out through the door.

"You did well," he tells me, "you always do.
You never make a mistake."
And I doze when he goes, only half asleep
while my nose is still wide awake.

BM

My Name is Lola

(for Liz)

I am Lola the labradoodle
My sense of smell is exquisite
I help my mistress when she's unwell
(A bit like a doctor's visit)
When her brain becomes fuzzy
Her actions get slow
I can smell something's wrong
Her blood sugar's too low
So I nudge her, or bark,
Or push her, or tug
Till she makes herself better
Then gives me a hug

For I'm Lola the Labradoodle
I'm a regular guy, just like you
It's just that my sense of smell is refined
It's just the job that I do

RS

Dogs in Parliament

If there was an election
to see who'd be top dog
in our village, I'd vote for...

the More Dog Biscuits in a Box party,

or the Ban All Cats from Our Street party,

or the Minimum Two Walks a Day party.

I might even stand for election myself
with policies such as...

All dogs should have the right to scratch carpets
or bark really loud when they feel like it.
All dogs should not be hosed down
when they roll in fox scat.
They should not be chastised
when they bring home trophy rats.

I'd have plenty of dogs
who'd vote for me,
plenty of dogs
who'd see in me
the kind of dog
who gets things done.

Dogs in Parliament?
Now that would be fun.
(And I do know for certain
that once there was one.)

*(The MP David Blunkett was blind and regularly brought
his guide dog to the House of Commons where she probably
managed to sleep through some very boring debates.)*

BM

Striker

I'm number nine
The star of the team
Pass me the ball
And watch me run
I wrong-foot the Welsh Terrier
I dribble round the Bulldog
Through the Dalmation's legs
Sell the Daschund a dummy
I'm heading for the goal
No one can catch me
Just the goalie to beat
A German Shepherd

He looks tough
He's heading towards me
I can hear the crowd cheering

Whoops!
I've burst the ball

RS

Museum

Would you like to visit
my museum?
The entry fee is
one rabbit-flavoured dog biscuit.

You'll enjoy the exhibits.
My favourite chewed-up rubber ring,
My old basket, with the tattered blanket,
Half a tennis ball,
A smelly stick,
A photo of my grandad, Frank the Labrador
and
My fossilised bone collection.

RS

FRANK

Why Don't You Love Me Any More?

Why don't you love me any more?
Why do you push me away?
You say, *Down boy!*
Moving back, as if the very thought
of having me near
is unbearable.
Why don't you love me any more?
Why, only five minutes ago
I was your favourite dog.
Have you forgotten already
how you threw my favourite red ball
across the garden?
How you laughed
as I bounded across the lawn
chasing its erratic dance
and dived into the pond
like an Olympic swimmer
making such a splash?
And now it seems
that just because I jumped onto your lap
all the fun we had means nothing.
Just because my coat is wet
and there's a slight drip and dribble on the carpet.
Why do you push me away?
Don't you love me any more?

RS

Is It Worth a Widdle?

For Lofty

Is it worth a widdle?
It's a question that concerns me.
Is this spot a place
where I should mark my territory?

The trees along the High Street
are always worth a drop.
A bus stop or a car wheel,
the bin outside the shop.

There are many different ways
to target a stream of pee.
and I can be acrobatic
with my delivery.

I can widdle from way down low,
I can widdle from a lofty height
and even when I'm out of wee
a fake widdle's still all right.

Other dogs watch enviously
but there really is no contest.
In any Widdling Olympics
they know I'd be the best.

So my advice is clear,
don't cause yourselves any stress.
Is it worth a widdle?
The answer's always – YES!

BM

Brambles

I'm quiet as a rule.
I don't like to stir things up.
I wouldn't say woof to a goose,
But there's one thing I can't resist –
Scrambling into a bramble bank,
Into that heady mess of spiky branches,
Into that bendy branchery of twisted twigginess
Redolent with the scent of rabbit.
For there you find the hidden pathways
Of the rabbit,
The burrows, hidden from view,
Where I can dig my paws into the soft earth
And tear at the trapped roots
After the divine prize,

And my man is calling me out,
But I pretend I can't hear
Because now my craving for rabbit
Is out of control.
And I know rabbit is near
As I scrabble the earth away,
Out of sight beneath the blackberries
And shiny green leaves.
And my man is calling.
I won't be long, I yell.
I'm so close, so close,
as I try to squeeze into the hole.

I can hear my man now,
crashing through the brambles.
His voice is cross.
Just a few minutes more, I yell.

That's all I need.
Just a few minutes more.

RS

My Teenage Years

My teenage years are over,
I've given up chewing shoes.
As for raiding the waste bin
and lunching on snotty tissues...

That wasn't me,
I'm sure I never did
anything like that.

My carpet-scratching was a phase
I won't return to again.
As for ripping a book
and chasing the hens...

That wasn't me,
I'm sure I never did
anything like that.

My food-stealing days are done with,
I don't do it any more.
And that badly scratched paint
on the kitchen door...

That wasn't me,
I'm sure I never did
anything like that.

Claw marks on the coffee table,
that must have been the cat.
And the vase that broke
and the mirror that cracked...

That wasn't me,
I'm sure I never did
anything like that.

You must believe me, please,
you can see it in my eyes.
Surely you know by now,
a labrador never lies!

BM

It's Your Fault

If you're going to leave the salmon
in clear view on the table
If you're going to leave the pie
on the window ledge
If you're going to leave
the bag of crisps on the sofa
If you're going to leave your supper
on the table, near the edge
If you're going to leave your favourite
biscuit on the tray
Well, you deserve to have it eaten
That's all I can say.

RS

Welsh Sheep Dog

Please don't confuse us
With the Border Collie
They are much too serious
We are far more jolly
We round up sheep and goats and cows
Through grass and trees and thistle
Those Border Collies have to wait
Until their owners whistle
We work out what needs doing
We are a brainy breed
We sort the sheep out from the goats
With our famous *joie-de-vivre*
We are the Welsh Sheep Dog
We're quick and make no fuss
If you've a job needs doing
You can rely on us

RS

Lost Balls

I must have been blessed
by the Patron Saint of Lost Balls,
as I seem to discover
all the ones that others
have left behind.

Nothing sweeter than finding
another dog's lost ball,
one that vanished into brambles,
till my mad scramble
recovered it.

I find balls from the village school
and those that the tennis club lose
when someone who thinks
he's a Wimbledon champ
ramps it up and over the wire.
(I leapt higher than ever
and caught one once
before it hit the ground!)

And then, if there's nothing new,
I'm happy to chew on whatever I find –
the manky ones, the mucky ones,
balls left to rot beneath the bushes.
Cricket balls, footballs,
I find them all, tear sponge balls
to shreds.

Don't mind if I get a mouthful
of mud, I'm just not worried
at all. There's such a feeling
of elation, such joyfulness,
such jubilation, when my nose
discovers, my paws uncover
yet another
lost ball.

BM

Secret

You can bribe me with treats
and biscuits and meats,
but I'm not telling you
where I buried it.
You can yell, you can shout,
you can stomp all about,
but I'm not telling you
where I buried it.
You can stroke me and tickle me
under my chin.
You can say, "Just you wait
till your mummy gets in."
You can offer me caviar
straight from the tin,
but I'm not telling you
where I buried it.
It's my favourite toy.
It's what gets my vote.
I just love to chew it.
It's what floats my boat.
I don't know what it's for
but it's called "a remote".
And I'm NOT telling you
where I buried it.

RS

Dog Show

I didn't win the *Obedience Class*
and *Most Gorgeous Golden Oldie* wasn't me.
I thought I stood a chance with *Longest Drool*
but the judges didn't agree.

I wasn't quick enough for the *Speediest Sit*
and a spaniel won *Best Paw Shaker*.
I thought I was a cert for *Fastest Sausage Eater*
but lost in the final tie-breaker.

Temptation Alley was too much to resist
and I mistimed the *Longest Stay Down*.
My *Appealing Expression* was appalling
when my face stayed set in a frown.

The Dog the Judges Would Like to Take Home
was never going to be me.
I wasn't scruffy enough for the *Scruffiest Dog*
and lost out to a mud-covered collie.

I wasn't *The Dog that Looks Like its Owner*
and *Most Fabulous Fella* was some other male.
But there was one class where I came in first…

I'm ***The Dog with the Waggiest Tail***.

BM

74

The Divorce Dog

They tell me I was the final straw
in a marriage going wrong.
They say that arguments and fights
had rumbled on for so long…

He said the house was small,
that two dogs were enough.
Talk of a third dog moving in
just got him in a huff.

Now I'm his reason for walking out,
I'm the cause of the split.
I'll always be the divorce dog,
the one that made him quit.

The Westie will stay with her
and the spaniel will go,
but what will happen to me
I honestly don't know.

I'll always be the break-up dog
each time she looks at me,
but a kiss-and-make-up dog
is what I'd really like to be.

BM

Call Me Lucky

My human's wonderful
He's really kind
I talk to other dogs
They get left alone
Neglected sometimes
But my human
He's with me all the time
He shares his food
And even sleeps with me
We have a special doorway
And I keep him warm at nights

I'm such a lucky dog

RS

The Things a Dog Has to Do

Clean the kitchen floor lest tiny scraps of food
    should spoil the appearance of the tiles.
Listen to the wind to mark a change in the weather.
Watch the cat carefully, lest her nerve breaks and
    she makes a dash for the window.

Remind potential burglars that she would make a
    fearsome adversary.
Check, by sniffing, that other dogs have clean
    bottoms.
Check, by sniffing, the four corners of the house
    for intruders.
Check, also by sniffing, the four corners of the
    garden for the same.
Seek the remnants of dead hedgehogs or other
    small animals and mark by rolling in them.
Watch the toy bone lest it move of its own accord.
Remind her owner, by subtle means, that it is time
    for a walk.
Remind her owner by less-subtle means that it is
    time to eat.
Bark loudly for no reason – just for the sheer joy
    of it.

Guard the front door lest the postman breaks in
    to steal a letter.
Wonder why the strange man who gave her
   the tasty bone is coming in through the window
   and not the door.

RS

Monsters

The Hoover Monster
Roaring and grumbling
Snarling and hissing
It's so
S C A R Y!

The Lawnmower Monster
Whirring and clanking
Clonking and whining
It's so
S C A R Y!!
It's so scary
if you're
a timid
little
dog
like
me

RS

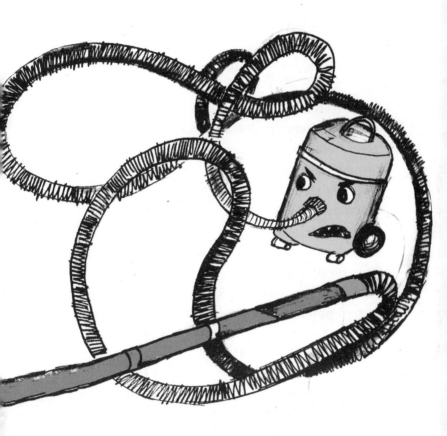

Rescue Dog

I come from a place
of bleakness and blindness,
somewhere across the sea.
I come from a place
of hurt and unkindness
where nobody wanted me.

I come from a place
where dogs were beaten
if they didn't do what they were told.
I come from a place
where my sleeping space
was outside in the cold.

I come from a place
where I fought for food,
where I dodged between kicking feet.
I come from a place
where sick dogs fell
and were left to die in the street.

So tell me again
that you realise
why my eyes are filled with fear.
Tell me again
that you understand
why I flinch when you come near.

Just give me
the time I need,
for my body and heart to heal.
Just give me
the space I need
to recover from my ordeal.

Then in time
I think I'll trust you,
you're different from the ones I knew.
In time
I may even accept
that there's kindness in what you do.

Your soft voice
helps me believe
you're someone who really will care.
Give me time,
give me space and warmth,
I've love inside me somewhere.

BM

Missing

I wonder where my human is,
I wonder where he's gone.
He left the house at half-past six.
He's not usually this long.
I hope he hasn't had a row
With the man from Number Four.
Perhaps he's ill or caught a chill,
Perhaps he's gone next door.
That's the home of Margaret.
They get on very well.
She always gives me doggy treats,
She has a lovely smell.
I wonder where my human is.
Now, I'm not one to fuss.
I hope he hasn't had a fall
Or been hit by a bus.
I expect that he'll be home quite soon
Because it's started raining.
His road sense isn't very good,
I think he needs more training.

I wonder if he took the car.
He's not much good at parking.
I think I'll climb the window seat
And try a bit of barking.
Ah, I can hear him coming now
And I know that it was wrong
To chew a hole in the sofa cover.

But he shouldn't have been so long!

RS

Moving House

I liked my house,
my spot by the radiator,
my place in the hall,
my seat in the window,
my basket under the stairs.

I liked my life in order.
I liked knowing what time we walked,
what time we played tug-of-war,
what time my food arrived.

But now it's changed.
And I didn't like
all the hustle and bustle,
all the crazy kerfuffle.

I didn't like how the house
was emptied of furniture
and boxes.
I didn't like having
nowhere to hide.

But I'm getting to like
my new house now,
my spot by the radiator,
my place in the hall,
my seat in the window,
my basket under the stairs.

And I get my walks,
and we're playing still
and my food
arrives on time.

I'm finding fresh places
to hide, and bit by bit,
smell by smell,
I'm thinking...

it's OK here.

BM

Hider

I'm a hider
I hide behind chairs
In the gap between the sofa and the wall
I can squeeze into tiny spaces
Behind the wardrobe
Between the dusty boxes under the bed
Anywhere it's dark
Any small and secret place
Under the stairs
In the garden behind the compost heap
Under the shed

My first man was scary
I don't like people
That's why I like to hide and sleep
Where it's dark and enclosed
Away from humans

But my new owners are kind
They are special
I sit with them on the sofa
And sometimes sleep on their bed
But I still feel happiest
Hiding

RS

Cheese

I like eating fish and chips
Scampi and mushy peas
Marrow bones and ice-cream cones
But my favourite treat is cheese
I like eating curry
Chow Mein from the Chinese
Dim Sum salvaged from the bin
But my favourite treat is cheese
Chicken skins – they're very good
I bet no one disagrees
And chicken fat and those gristly bits
But my favourite treat is cheese
I'm quite partial to parsnip
And the acquired taste of fleas
And stale bread from beneath my bed
But my favourite treat is cheese
I love to chew up trainers
And Duncan's dungarees
And Franny's frocks and Grandpa's socks
But my favourite treat is cheese
I'm a connoisseur of fine dining
I have a gourmet's expertise
I like oysters and caviar and Duck à l'Orange
But my favourite treat is cheese

RS

Old Black Dog

Did you ever see such an old black dog?

A laze about in the warm French sun dog.
A pat me if you like
but you won't make me get up and run dog.
A once upon a time
I'd play with a ball in the park dog.
A now I'm too tired and I can't be bothered to bark
dog.

A cats don't worry me like they used to dog,
but if one of them invades my space
I'll still show it a thing or two dog,
A don't expect me to hear when you call dog,
a leave me to dream and let me sprawl dog.

A scratch my tummy,
look for me where it's sunny
dog.

BM

Stick

It might seem obvious to you humans
But it puzzles me every day
If you want the stick so badly
Why do you throw it away?

RS

The Invisible Dog

There'll be the scent of sadness
when you think I've gone away.
And you won't know where I am,
the silent sofa will not say.

In the rustle of the leaves
there will, of course, be clues,
a ripple in the flowers,
a sniff around your shoes.

I'll be the bark that startles you,
the shuffle behind your back.
I'll be the snuffle at your door,
the stroll along the track.

No need for food or water,
or to work out where to wee.
None of these things concern me now
I'm invisible, can't you see?

No need to try and understand
all of those words you say.
No need to watch as you stumble
each time I lie in your way.

Just seek me in the shadows
when the day is almost done,
a blur, a sigh, a flash of fur,
an invisible dog on the run.

BM

95

About the Poets and the Illustrator

Brian Moses has worked as a professional poet since 1988 and performs his poetry and percussion shows in schools, libraries, theatres and festivals around the UK and abroad. When asked by CBBC to write a poem for the Queen's 80th birthday he wrote a poem about her corgis. He has published many children's poetry collections, as well as books written with Roger Stevens, including *Olympic Poems, What Are We Fighting For?* and *1066 and Before That*. Brian lives in East Sussex with his wife and their fox-red Labrador called Honey.

His website is: www.brianmoses.co.uk and he blogs at brian-moses.blogspot.com

Roger Stevens visits schools, libraries and festivals, performing his work and running workshops for young people and teachers. He is a National Poetry Day Ambassador and runs the award-winning poetry website www.poetryzone.co.uk for children and teachers. He has published over thirty books of poetry for children, including the collections authored with Brian Moses. He spends his time between the Loire, in France, and Brighton, where he lives with his wife and his very shy dog, Jasper.

Ed Boxall has written and illustrated several books, such as *Mr Trim and Miss Jumble* and *Dolphins Keep Me Safe in Dreams*. He performs his stories and poems with music, projections, and lots of joining in. Edboxall.com

Bloody Kiss

Chapitre 1

ET PUIS QUOI, ENCORE ?!

TUER...

BOM

RÂA

AH

MAÎTRE KURO-BOSHI !

TU N'Y ES PAS ALLÉE DE MAIN MORTE...

J'AURAIS DÛ ME MÉFIER.

VOUS DEVRIEZ FAIRE ATTENTION ! VOUS ÊTES TOUT JUSTE AUSSI FORT QU'UN HUMAIN, EN CE MOMENT.

C'EST QUI, LUI ?!

KIYO KATSURAGI !

QU'EST-CE QUE TU FAIS ?

FWAAH

RIEN DU TOUT...

R...

BON !

URGH

ÇA SE MANGE ?

BLUSH

Ha ha ha ha ha !

JE COMPRENDRAIS QUE TU N'EN VEUILLES PAS !

...

EUH...

CE N'EST PAS SPÉCIALEMENT POUR TE REMERCIER POUR HIER.

JE NE SAIS PAS CE QUE MANGENT LES VAMPIRES...

J'AI UN PEU TOUT LOUPÉ, MAIS BON...

TIENS.

T...

DONNE-LE-MOI !

CE FUT LA SEULE À ACCEPTER DE NOUS SAUVER SANS AVOIR PEUR DE NOUS.

ELLE NOUS A RECUEILLIS.

NOUS ÉTIONS POURSUIVIS PAR NOTRE CLAN ET N'AVIONS NULLE PART OÙ NOUS RÉFUGIER.

IL SERAIT TRÈS PÉNIBLE POUR NOUS DE QUITTER CETTE MAISON.

D'AILLEURS...

LE PÈRE DE MAÎTRE KUROBOSHI EST UN VAMPIRE ET SA MÈRE EST UNE HUMAINE.

QUOI ?

C'EST UN DHAMPIRE, UN ÊTRE MI-HOMME, MI-VAMPIRE.

NOUS AVONS DÉJÀ DU MAL À SUPPORTER LA PERTE DE MADAME MINÉKO.

IL S'EST MIS À HAÏR SON CÔTÉ HUMAIN.

À CAUSE D'EUX...

OUI...

LES MEMBRES DU CLAN LE TENAIENT À L'ÉCART À CAUSE DE SON SANG HUMAIN.

C'EST POUR ÇA...

C'EST SI TRISTE.

D'ÊTRE TOUTE SEULE...

JE SAIS CE QUE C'EST D'ÊTRE REJETÉ...

AAH-
AH!

ZZZ SSS...

DE QUOI VOUS PARLEZ ?

CRITCH

ET COMME IL DÉTESTAIT LES HUMAINS, IL N'ESSAYAIT MÊME PAS DE S TROUVER UNE FIANCÉE...

ON A ENVIE DE TROUVER UNE PLACE DANS LA VIE.

QUAND IL A DÉCLARÉ QU'IL VOUS VOULAIT POUR ÉPOUSE, ÇA M'A ÉTONNÉ...

ON EN VIENT À SE DEMANDER...

MAIS TU M'AS FAIT PEUR !

EUH...

C'était pas la peine de déchirer mon t-shirt...

À QUOI SERT CETTE EXISTENCE...

WOUAH ?!

SWIP

Oh ! Joli ! ♥

Bonjour à tous, c'est Kazuko Furumiya. Merci beaucoup d'avoir acheté le premier volume de «Bloody Smack» (ainsi renommé par Seiko Nakamura*). J'espère que vous prendrez plaisir à le lire !

Ce manga qui devait être une histoire courte en un seul volume s'est transformé en série. Et je dois avouer que la qualité des chapitres est assez inégale du point de vue des dessins... Surtout le premier chapitre...
Lors de la parution dans le magazine, c'était vraiment la catastrophe... J'ai essayé de l'améliorer un peu pour l'édition en volumes reliés. À vrai dire, Kiyo (l'héroïne) n'avait pas le même uniforme dans le chapitre 1. J'espère que ça se voit moins maintenant, j'ai fait en sorte d'apporter un peu d'unité à sa tenue !
(Il faudrait que je corrige ça pour ma prochaine édition...)
Cet uniforme est très pénible à dessiner mais il me plaît bien. Ça m'amuse beaucoup de dessiner les vêtements de mes personnages féminins, en particulier les uniformes (je suis un peu tordue...)
À contrario, les garçons... ça ne m'intéresse pas tant que ça de les habiller... (À part les uniformes, bien sûr <= je suis vraiment tordue...)

* Auteur du manga *Yujo Survival*, publié dans le même magazine que *Bloody Kiss*.

Furumiya a tendance à redessiner la même case des millions de fois ! Que ce soit pour le story-board, pour les esquisses au crayon ou pour le passage à l'encre.

Par exemple dans le chapitre 2, la 3e case de la page 66 : je l'ai recommencée tellement de fois qu'à la fin, j'en avais les larmes aux yeux.

À suivre page 102.

Baigné par la lumière naissante de la lune...

une ombre mouvante
semble déchirer la nuit...

Comme chaque soir, il se met en chasse
du sang pur d'une jeune vierge.

SUITE À UN CONCOURS DE CIRCONSTANCES, JE ME SUIS RETROUVÉE À VIVRE AVEC EUX...

J'AI HÉRITÉ DE MA GRAND-MÈRE UNE IMMENSE MAISON...

HABITÉE PAR DEUX VAMPIRES.

ÇA M'A FAIT SUPER MAL ET SI TU RECOMMENCES, JE RISQUE DE FINIR ANÉMIÉE.

TU AS BU MON SANG UNE FOIS, C'EST TOUT !

Hé ho !

DEPUIS, JE PASSE MON TEMPS À FAIRE DES TÂCHES MÉNAGÈRES.

LA PROCHAINE FOIS, J'IRAI DOUCEMENT.

UNE FOIS SUFFIT POUR QUE VOUS DEVENIEZ SA FIANCÉE.

...ROBOSHI EST ...DHAMPIRE... ...TIÉ HUMAIN, ...TIÉ VAMPIRE. IL ...NT TRÈS FAIBLE ...ND IL NE BOIT ...S DE SANG.

GRIP

ET UNE FOIS QU'UN VAMPIRE A CHOISI SA MOITIÉ, IL NE PEUT PLUS BOIRE QUE SON SANG.

AÏE.

CE SONT DES INSTANTS PRIVILÉGIÉS.

PLONK
じょぼー————ん...

BON...

EN GROS, ON EST...

PAUVRES.

LE MANOIR TOMBE EN RUINE.

ON S'EST DONNÉ DU MA MAIS AU FINA C'EST PLUTÔ FRUGAL.

On n'y peut rien...
ON N'A PAS BEAUCOUP D'ARGENT, JE DOIS ÉCONO- MISER SUR LA NOURRITURE.

PLITCH

VOILÀ TOUT...

Sardine carboni- sée par Kiyo.

← Fuite.

CROC

TU M'EMPÊCHES DE FAIRE MON TRAVAIL, RENTRE À LA MAISON !

AÏE !

N'OUBLIE PAS...

QUE TU ES MA FIANCÉE...

QU'EST-CE QUE JE VAIS FAIRE ?

J'ESPÈRE QU'IL N'A DÉRANGÉ PERSONNE...

IE NE PENSAIS
G QU'IL VIENDRAIT
TTRE SON GRAIN
SEL JUSQU'ICI...

NE REMETS PAS LES PIEDS ICI DEMAIN !

TOC

ça va aller ?

Regardez un peu les vêtements de Kuroboshi... On dirait qu'il porte une combinaison moulante... Ça me rappelle quelqu'un...

JE VEUX VITE DEVENIR... HUMAIN (ero)*

Ce pauvre Kuroboshi va bientôt devenir un membre à part entière de ce groupe d'hommes démons... Je n'y peux rien, je n'arrive pas à imaginer de tenue originale pour lui. Ça ne m'intéresse pas ! Mais la combinaison moulante, c'est vraiment trop... Donc j'ai fait un petit effort pour le chapitre 3. Évidemment, ça m'a pris plus de temps que d'habitude. Kuroboshi a maintenant acquis le pouvoir de transformation de type uniforme ! (allez savoir ce que ça veut dire...) À partir du chapitre 4, il adopte l'uniforme pour de bon. Je me suis bien amusée à le dessiner !

J'ai fait une page de titre en couleur d'avance... Mais là aussi, il y avait un piège...

*Référence à une réplique célèbre des personnages de la série *Yokai Ningen Bem* ("Bem l'homme démon").

IL EST VRAIMENT INTRUSIF, CE GARÇON...

ELLE NE CHERCHE MÊME PAS À SAVOIR CE QUE JE RESSENS.

QUOI ?

Waouh...

KIYO, LE BEAU GARÇON D'HIER EST REVENU.

IL EST VRAIMENT REVENU !!

JE LUI AVAIS POURTANT DIT DE NE PLUS REMETTRE LES PIEDS ICI !

HI HI!

ARRÊTE DE DIRE DES BÊTISES ET VA-T'EN !

TU T'ES DÉCIDÉE À DÉMISSIONNER ?

QU'EST-CE QU'IL A DERRIÈRE LA TÊTE ?!

MAINTENANT QUE VOUS ÊTES LÀ, TOI ET ARCHE...

CE N'EST PAS GRAND-CHOSE...

MAIS JE VAIS FAIRE TOUT MON POSSIBLE...

EN CETTE SAISON, C'EST PARFAIT POUR DE L'ODEN* !

ET QUAND J'AI DEMANDÉ CE QU'ON POUVAIT PRÉPARER AVEC DU RADIS BLANC, LE MARCHAND M'A RÉPONDU...

* Bouillon de légumes et de pâtés de poissons, plat typique de l'hiver.

QUAND IL M'A DIT ÇA...

JE ME SUIS SOUVENUE QUE J'EN AVAIS MANGÉ DANS LE TEMPS, AVEC MA FAMILLE...

L'ODEN, C'EST DÉLICIEUX.

MAIS IL FAUT EN PRÉPARER BEAUCOUP À LA FOIS...

ET QUAND J'ÉTAIS SEULE, JE N'AI PLUS JAMAIS EU L'OCCASION D'EN MANGER.

MAIS...

SI C'EST TOI QUI LE PRÉPARES, ÇA VA ENCORE CRAMER...

J'AI HÂTE D'Y GOÛTER...

ON POURRA EN MANGER ENSEMBLE !

POUR ARRIVER À ÊTRE HEUREUSE.

TIENS ?

À PARTIR DU LENDEMAIN, KUROBOSHI N'EST PLUS JAMAIS REVENU AU RESTAURANT.

JE ME DEMANDE POURQUOI...

KUROBOSHI, COME BACK !

MAIS COMME KUROBOSHI ATTEND BEAUCOUP DE MOI...

JE SUIS PEUT-ÊTRE UN PEU SIMPLISTE ...

MERCI !

BON COURAGE, KIYO !

Sur le chemin du lycée.

PAR ICI, JE VOUS PRIE.

OUI, NE VOUS INQUIÉTEZ PAS !

TU VEUX TRAVAILLER ENCORE PLUS ? TU ES SÛRE QUE ÇA VA ALLER ?

ÇA ME POUSSE À FAIRE DES EFFORTS.

FWAAH!

ALLEZ, RENTRONS.

Ah !

OUI.

JE VAIS FAIRE TOUT MON POSSIBLE.

ET·JE POURRAI CUISINER POUR KUROBOSHI...

JE TOUCHERAI MA PAYE DEMAIN !

HaaS

KIYO, TU ES TRÈS PÂLE. TU NE VEUX PAS RENTRER PLUS TÔT, CE SOIR ?

AA-AH !

IL FAUT QUE JE SOIS FORTE... ET QUE JE FASSE MON BOULOT À FOND.

NON, ÇA VA !

ET JE VAIS ME RÉCONCILIER AVEC KUROBOSHI.

QU...

ARCHE M'A DIT QUE TU SERAIS GUÉRI SI TU BUVAIS DU SANG !

ALORS...

JE NE
PEUX RIEN
TE REFUSER.

PFF...

VRAIMENT...

NOUS AVONS UNE SURPRISE POUR FÊTER VOTRE RÉTABLISSEMENT, MAÎTRE KUROBOSHI.

AAA-RGH !!

C'EST DE L'ODEN !

MLLE KIYO A PRÉPARÉ UNE MARMITE CARBONISÉE !

Restes du 3e jour.

TU VAS FAIRE DE L'ODEN PENDANT ENCORE COMBIEN DE JOURS ?

DEMAIN, JE RÉUSSIRAI ! VOUS ALLEZ VOIR !

TOC

JE VAIS AU LYCÉE.

Livre de cuisine.

Croquis refusés pour la page 66

N°1 et n°2 : L'angle de vue n'était pas bon. Les esquisses n'avaient pas une position naturelle.

N°3 : Je n'aime pas du tout celui-ci. Kuroboshi est chauve. On dirait une drôle de mascotte posée sur l'épaule de Kiyo.

N°4 : Refusé car il n'était pas assez percutant. Avec le recul, j'ai complètement raté les jambes...

N°5 : La scène devient trop érotique sans raison...

Voilà pourquoi j'ai mis plus de 10 heures à finaliser la page 66. C'est malin !

Un petit exercice de style : Kiyo en garçon et Kuroboshi en fille. Kiyo serait un garçon appliqué et sérieux ! Kuroboshi serait une jolie fille capricieuse et effrontée. Le changement de sexe ne va pas tellement à Kiyo, mais Kuroboshi est presque mieux en fille !

CES ROSES SONT AUSSI L'HÉRITAGE DE MA GRAND-MÈRE !

Pourquoi j'en suis réduit à ça ?

Arrachage des mauvaises herbes.

ELLE A RAISON.

IL FAUT EN PRENDRE SOIN.

ET SON SERVITEUR, ARCHE.

VOICI KUROBOSHI.

ET BIEN S'EN OCCUPER POUR AVOIR UN MAGNIFIQUE JARDIN.

Et bon appétit, bien sûr...

TU AS UNE ÉTRANGE CONCEPTION DU MOT PRÉCIEUX !

LE THÉ À LA ROSE, LA CONFITURE DE ROSE, LES BAGELS À LA ROSE SONT DES ALIMENTS TRÈS PRÉCIEUX.

IL FAUT LES TRAITER AVEC RESPECT.

FAIS-MOI VOIR.

Je me suis piquée sur une épine...

ZUT...

AÏE !

C'EST PAS MA FAUTE SI ON EST PAUVRES !

TIC

JE VAIS TE LÉCHER LE DOIGT POUR TE SOIGNER.

CETTE MANIE DE FRAPPER SANS PRÉVENIR...

BONG

S... STOP !

108

TIENS ?

MA PIQÛRE...

EN ASPIRANT TON SANG...

JE PEUX AUSSI FAIRE CE GENRE DE CHOSES.

FFF...

MER... Bon, puisque c'est gentiment offert...

HI HI HI

PAS MAL, HEIN ?

Mais... Débile !

VOUS ÉTIEZ LES SEULS À VOUS FAIRE DES MAMOURS, JE VOULAIS PARTICIPER...

C'EST PAS À TOI QUE JE L'AI OFFERTE !

Allez !

VENEZ PRENDRE LE PETIT-DÉJEUNER.

MERCI BEAUCOUP !

ILS SONT UN PEU TURBULENTS...

Il faut toujours l'avoir à l'œil.

NE LE LAISSE PAS TE LA REPRENDRE.

MAIS JE M'AMUSE BIEN, AVEC EUX.

111

Les couleurs de Kuro-
boshi sont le noir et le
rouge. Plein de noir et
plein de rouge partout !
Tiens ? J'ai déjà vu ça
quelque part...

TU M'AS
FRAPPÉ !
ALORS QUE
MÊME MON
PÈRE...*
(ETC.)

Même son uniforme
ressemble à celui de
cette série de mecha...
Peut-être Kuroboshi va-
t-il se transformer un
jour en pilote d'armure
mobile...

Il se peut que ces
robots géants aient
trop influencé mon
imaginaire...

Pour finir, je vous donne
mon adresse au cas où
vous auriez envie de
m'écrire vos impres-
sions sur ma série !

Kazuko Furumiya
Éditions Glénat
Immeuble Diderot
39 rue du gouverneur-
général-Éboué
92130
Issy les Moulineaux

* Référence à une réplique célèbre
d'un personnage de *Gundam*.

ET ELLE...
ELLE AVAIT UN
UNIFORME DU
LYCÉE TOMEI,
NON ?

IL Y A DES
ÉLÈVES QUI
VONT À CE
LYCÉE EN
VÉLO ?

C'EST UNE
ÉCOLE POUR
RICHES.

OH ?
QUEL EST CE
BRUIT ?

À CE SOIR,
MADEMOISELL

DÉSOLÉE, LE ROND-POINT ÉTAIT BOUCHÉ.

Ah...

Bonne journée...

HEIN ?

2 heures 15.

Ouf...

J'AI BATTU MON RECORD.

ÉBERLUÉS

UN BAL ?

GRAND BAL EN L'HONNEUR DE L'ANNIVERSAIRE DU LYCÉE

S'ILS ONT ENVIE DE S'AMUSER, ILS N'ONT QU'À ORGANISER UNE JOURNÉE DÉTERRAGE DE POMMES DE TERRE !...

Elle est là grâce à sa bourse.

JE NE COMPRENDS PAS COMMENT FONCTIONNENT LES RICHES.

NOUS ALLONS AUJOURD'HUI DÉSIGNER LES ÉLÈVES QUI SERONT CHARGÉS D'ORGANISER LE BAL.

POURQUOI LA FORCER ?

KOBAYASHI N'A PAS L'AIR RAVIE DE SON RÔLE.

TU AS QUELQUE CHOSE À DIRE ?

K... Katsu-ragi ?!

QU'EST-CE QUE TU ME VEUX ?!

QU...

EUH...

QUAND JE VOIS QUELQU'UN SE FAIRE AGRESSER, JE NE PEUX PAS M'EMPÊCHER DE LE DÉFENDRE.

QUOI ?

JE VAIS LE FAIRE.

JE VOULAIS JUSTE TERMINER CETTE RÉUNION AU PLUS VITE.

TU AS MIEUX À PROPOSER ?

ET VOILÀ, UN PRÊTÉ POUR UN RENDU.

Quelle inso-lence !

JE M'OCCUPERAI DE L'ORGANISATION.

VOILÀ LE BUDGET POUR LA MISE EN SCÈNE.

BON...

GRAND BAL · RÉUNION DES ORGANISATEURS

JE ME DEMANDE QUELLE SERAIT LA RÉACTION DE KUROBOSHI S'IL APPRENAIT ÇA...

IDIO-TE

OUI, JE SAIS, LE BUDGET EST TRÈS SERRÉ CETTE ANNÉE.

EUH... IL NE MANQUE PAS UN ZÉRO, LÀ ?

Mais...

J'AI OUBLIÉ MON DÉJEUNER !

Bon, je vais manger.

TU PARLES D'UNE CORVÉE.

ESSAYEZ DE RÉFLÉCHIR À UNE MISE EN SCÈNE MARQUANTE À MOINDRES FRAIS.

Je vais sauter le repas de midi... JE N'AI PAS D'ARGENT POUR ACHETER UN SANDWICH...

BOUH...

EUH...

C'EST VOTRE TRAVAIL.

FIXE

D'ACCORD, ON VA DANS LA COUR ?

EUH… KOBAYASHI, C'EST ÇA ?

SI ÇA NE TE DÉRANGE PAS, TU VEUX BIEN QU'ON DÉJEUNE ENSEMBLE ?

JE SUIS DÉSOLÉE POUR CE QUI T'ARRIVE, C'EST MA FAUTE…

MAIS NON, TU N'Y ES POUR RIEN.

Si tu veux…

TU POURRAIS M'AIDER DANS LES PRÉPARATIFS.

TU ES SÛRE ?

MERCI, ÇA ME SAUVE LA VIE !

C'EST UNE GENTILLE FILLE…

AVEC PLAISIR !

K...

KURO-BOSHI ?!

SA-LUT !

AH, JE TE TROUVE ENFIN.

QU...

QU'EST-CE QUE TU VIENS FAIRE ICI ?!

C'EST PAS LA PORTE À CÔTÉ, TON LYCÉE...

ÉPUISE

OOH !

POM

TIENS !

MERCI...

IL EST VENU EXPRÈS ME L'APPORTER ?

T'avais pas l'impression qu'il te manquait quelque chose ?

TU AVAIS OUBLIÉ ÇA, CE MATIN.

119

Ne dis pas ça...

LE COURANT PASSE BIEN, ENTRE VOUS...

SURTOUT KUROBOSHI, IL A L'AIR DE T'AIMER TRÈS FORT...

EUH... KOBAYASHI...

HA HA HA !

EXCUSE-LE !

PAS DEVANT TOUT LE MONDE !

MAIS NON !

QUELLE MERVEILLEUSE HISTOIRE D'AMOUR...

TU CONNAIS LA RUMEUR...

QUI ENTOURE LE BAL DU LYCÉE ?

Zut...

ELLE SE FAIT DES IDÉES, MAINTENANT...

MOI, JE ME SUIS PROMIS D'ALLER AU BAL AVEC MON MEILLEUR AMI D'ENFANCE.

ON N'EST PAS AUSSI PROCHES QUE VOUS DEUX, MAIS...

MON RÊVE SERAIT QU'IL M'ARRIVE LA MÊME CHOSE.

IL Y A TRÈS LONGTEMPS, UN ÉLÈVE DU LYCÉE...

A DEMANDÉ SA PETITE AMIE EN MARIAGE PENDANT LE BAL.

JE SAIS !

ET SI POUR LA MISE EN SCÈNE, ON SE BASAIT SUR CETTE LÉGENDE ?

IL LUI A OFFERT UNE ROSE POUR FAIRE SA DEMANDE...

PENDANT LE BAL, LES COUPLES S'ÉCHANGERAIENT DES ROSES !

ET AU LIEU DE RÉPONDRE "OUI", SA PETITE AMIE A ACCEPTÉ EN LUI RENDANT SA ROSE...

JE VAIS PRENDRE MON COURAGE À DEUX MAINS...

C'EST UN PEU PAR HASARD QUE JE SUIS DEVENUE ORGANISATRICE DE CE BAL...

C'EST UNE MAGNIFIQUE IDÉE !

DES ROSES EN PAPIER FAITES À LA MAIN, CE SERAIT CHARMANT !

Waah !

COMME ON A PEU DE BUDGET IL FAUDRAIT FAIRE DES ROSES EN PAPIER !

HEEIN ?!

CE SERA POUR TOI L'OCCASION PARFAITE DE FAIRE TA DÉCLARATION.

Comment as-tu deviné ?!

OOOH !

MAIS JE VAIS FAIRE DE MON MIEUX POUR QU'IL SOIT RÉUSSI !

Kuroboshi...

Pourquoi m'as-tu donné un coup de poing ?

OOH !

REGARDEZ !

UNE ROSE GÉANTE !!

L'EX-PLOSION DE MON ART !

JE VOULAIS SIMPLEMENT AIDER UN PEU MLLE KIYO...

C'est pour ça que j'ai mis un tablier.

Je n'en ai pas l'air, mais je suis assez habile de mes mains.

AAAH !

PAS TOUUU-CHE !

Bon-jour !

MAIS LAISSEZ-MOI VOUS SALUER D'UN BAISEMAIN.

ROGER !

Si je puis me per-mettre.

Pff...

Elle est trop grosse, on ne p[...] rien en faire.

BON, ON SE RÉPARTIT LES FEUILLES ET ON FINIT ÇA EN VITESSE.

C'ÉTAIT ÇA, LA CHUTE ?

ET VOILÀ.

Bande de méchants...

SCELLÉ

ELLE A PERSÉVÉRÉ JUSQU'À ÉPUISEMENT...

NE BAISSE PAS LES BRAS ! JE VAIS T'AIDER.

SNIF

QUELLE IDIOTE...

MAÎTRE KUROBOSHI.

VOUS NE TROUVEZ PAS QUE Mlle KIYO RESSEMBLE BEAUCOUP À MADAME MINÉKO ?

QUOI ?

JE CROIS QUE JE ME SUIS HEURTÉE À UN OBSTACLE DE TAILLE...

QUAND NOUS SOMMES ARRIVÉS DANS CETTE DEMEURE...

IL Y AVAIT UNE ROSERAIE DONT MADAME MINÉKO PRENAIT GRAND SOIN...

NE FAITES RIEN DE RÉPRÉHENSIBLE !

JE VAIS LA PORTER DANS SON LIT.

JE N'ARRIVE PAS À ME PASSER D'ELLE.

DE TOUTE FAÇON, ELLE SE DÉFEND DANS SON SOMMEIL.

FWAP

zz

BAM

AU FINAL, LES HUMAINS ET NOUS…

…

NOUS NE SOMMES PAS SI DIFFÉRENTS.

ELLE EST EN RETARD.

En plus…

Qu'est-ce qu'elle fabrique…

PSS…

Débris.

ÇA NE VA PAS DU TOUT… KOBAYASHI M'ENCOURAGE, MAIS JE N'Y ARRIVE TOUJOURS PAS…

WOUAH

CRITCH !!

CRITCH !!

CRITCH !!

CRITCH !!

POUR-
QUOI ?!

TOUT EST FICHU ?

J'AI MIS TELLEMENT DE TEMPS À PLIER TOUTES CES FLEURS...

FWAAH...

À LA MAISON...

IL N'Y A MÊME PAS MILLE ROSES DANS CE JARDIN, IDIOTE !!

IL FAUT QUE JE CUEILLE MILLE ROSES POUR DEMAIN.

MES ROSES ONT ÉTÉ SABOTÉES.

QU'EST-CE QUE TU FAIS ICI ?!

FWAP

TU DOIS LES CUEILLIR POUR DEMAIN ?

TOUTES LES ROSES ONT ÉCLOS EN MÊME TEMPS !!

KURO-BOSHI !

TIENS.

JE M'INQUIÉTAIS DE NE PAS TE VOIR ARRIVER.

Euh...

JE SUIS DÉSOLÉE...

KOBAYASHI !

BONNE CHANCE.

MERCI, KATSURAGI.

C'ÉTAIT DE LA TENDRESSE...

JE ME SOUVIENS ENCORE DE CE QUE J'AVAIS RESSENTI CE JOUR-LÀ...

QUAND TU ES TRISTE, JE LE SUIS AUSSI.

ELLE N'EST PAS OBLIGÉE DE PRENDRE SOIN DES AUTRES COMME ELLE LE FAIT.

ET AUSSI...

DE L'IMPATIENCE.

ELLE EST...

SI MALADROITE...

MÊME SI ON LA PIÉTINE, ELLE TIENT BON.

CETTE
PETITE FLEUR.

N...

NOO-ON !

ELLE N'A PAS MÉNAGÉ SES EFFORTS.

EN LOQUES

Oui !

Ho ho ho !

NOTRE PETITE BLAGUE NE L'A PAS EMPÊCHÉE DE SE RIDICULISER.

VOUS AVEZ VU DANS QUEL ÉTAT ÉTAIT KIYO KATSURAGI ?

BLA

Tiens ?

QUI EST-CE ?

ELLE ME PLAÎT COMME ÇA.

JE T'AIME.

Bloody Kiss I / Fin

La neige d'un blanc immaculé qui volait autour de lui semblait former des ailes.

L'histoire qui va suivre s'est passée trois jours avant Noël...

J'AI VRAIMENT CRU QUE C'ÉTAIT UN ANGE TOMBÉ DU CIEL...

La chute du siècle.

EUH...

ARGH

HE HE !

TELLEMENT PEUR QUE J'AI FAILLI AVOIR UNE CRISE CARDIAQUE !!

JE T'AI FAIT PEUR ?

C'ÉTAIT UNE BLAGUE !

N...

NOOON !!

POUCE ! POUUUCE...

BON, OK.

J'AVAIS PAS ENVIE D'ÊTRE TOUT SEUL POUR NOËL, EN PLUS.*

JE VEUX BIEN FAIRE ÉQUIPE AVEC TOI.

JE RIGOLAIS.

*Japon, Noël est considéré comme la fête des amoureux.

GRAB

MERCIII !

C'EST VRAI ?!

Ah oui, au fait...

ÇA FAIT COMBIEN DE TEMPS QUE TU JOUES DE LA GUITARE ?

BEN QUOI ? C'EST TOI QUI M'AS SAUTÉ DESSUS.

...

JE SUIS PAS GUITARISTE.

FWAAA!

AH !

SHINJI TENSHI

22 FÉVRIER

PERMIS DE CONDUIRE

JANVIER 1998

CONDITIONS D'UTILISATION

EXCELLENT

UN PERMIS DE MOTO ?

FRSSH

Le sac d'Angel.

TENSHI*?!

*Ange en japonais.

ZUT...

Oh...

VLIP

HMM ....

GRIP

IL A 16 ANS... UN AN DE MOINS QUE MOI.

IL S'APPELLE VRAIMENT "ANGE"...

QUEL HASARD !!

QUI EST-IL EN RÉALITÉ ?

JE PENSE QU'IL ÉTAIT DANS LA MUSIQUE...

Je ne peux pas apprendre grand-chose avec ce permis...

CHANTE, MIZUHO !

OK !!

MERCI, ANGEL.

UN GROUPE INDÉPENDANT TRÈS CONNU DANS LE KANSAI, ILS SONT NUMBER ONE.

ÇA Y EST, JE ME SOUVIENS. C'EST LE CHANTEUR DE "SERAPH"...

MAIS J'AVAIS ENTENDU DIRE QU'ILS DEVAIENT FAIRE LEURS DÉBUTS EN TANT QUE PROS AUJOURD'HUI, POUR NOËL.

TU AS VU ÇA ?

?

J'AI L'IMPRESSION D'AVOIR FAIT LE PREMIER PAS POUR ALLER DE L'AVANT...

ILS ONT L'AIR DE S'ÉCLATER, TOUS LES DEUX.

WAAAH

C'EST PAS VRAI...

VAINQUEUR : EXALTED ANGEL !

La chambre de Kazuko

Bon ...

en gros, je n'ai pas d'idée pour remplir ces pages.

Bienvenue à tous dans la chambre de Kazuko.

Ces pages bonus vont me servir à vous décrire mon quotidien monotone et inintéressant.

Si ça vous ennuie, vous n'êtes pas obligés de lire tout ça.

ET N'OUBLIE PAS D'ARROSER LES PLANTES !

OUI.

Et voilà comment elle m'a confié de nombreuses tâches pendant son absence.

J'espère sincèrement que mes parents vont vivre vieux.

OUI. (SÛREMENT PAS)

OUI. (PEUT-ÊTRE)

PRÉPARE-TOI DE VRAIS REPAS.

ET FAIS BIEN LE MÉNAGE.

Un jour, ma mère a dû se faire hospitaliser.

JE N'AI PAS LA MAIN VERTE POUR DEUX SOUS...

AAAH...

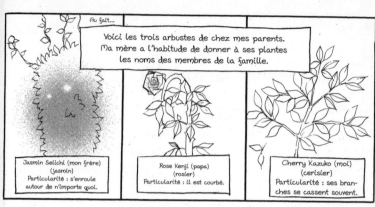

Au fait...

Voici les trois arbustes de chez mes parents.
Ma mère a l'habitude de donner à ses plantes
les noms des membres de la famille.

Jasmin Seiichi (mon frère)
(jasmin)
Particularité : s'enroule
autour de n'importe quoi.

Rose Kenji (papa)
(rosier)
Particularité : il est courbé.

Cherry Kazuko (moi)
(cerisier)
Particularité : ses branches se cassent souvent.

ZUT...
SEIICHI
EST
FANÉ !!

Marron

Un jour...

Je les ai oubliés.

Waah !

Mais à l'approche de la date de bouclage...

En le voyant pousser, maman avait déclaré...

JE VOULAIS AVOIR UN MIGNON PETIT ROSIER NAIN, MAIS IL A GRANDI ET GRANDI ENCORE !

Bon courage, Kenji !

Il a fleuri.

Je l'ai aussitôt arrosé, et à partir de ce moment, je me suis un peu plus intéressée au sort de ces pauvres plantes.

À commencer par Rose Kenji.

Il a des fleurs superbes mais il est bizarrement tordu...

Mais on dirait qu'il fuit Kazuko et Kenji.

Je commence à comprendre pourquoi mon petit frère est parti vivre à Tokyo...

Pression

Il s'enroule autour de tout ce qui est à proximité.

Séchoir à linge.

Ensuite, Jasmin Seiichi.

Il est plutôt coriace, malgré son air désinvolte.

Comme on était au début de l'été, elle donnait pas mal de fruits.

OH !

Et pour finir, Cherry Kazuko. Je me sens proche d'elle, sûrement parce qu'on a le même nom.

Ça fait 4 ans que je suis devenue mangaka. Il s'est passé plein de choses entre-temps.

ELLE N'AVAIT DONNÉ QU'UNE SEULE CERISE, L'ANNÉE DERNIÈRE.

ET SES BRANCHES N'ARRÊTAIENT PAS DE SE CASSER, JE ME SUIS MÊME DEMANDÉ COMMENT ELLE AVAIT FAIT POUR PASSER L'HIVER.

Quand j'y pense...

ET PENDANT CE TEMPS, JE FAISAIS XXX....

JE NE SAIS MÊME PLUS LE NOMBRE DE STORY-BOARDS QUI ONT ÉTÉ REFUSÉS. MACHIN M'A DIT XXX...

189

Moi aussi...

je devrais prendre exemple sur lui...

Ce dessin n'est qu'un symbole.

Mais...

cet arbrisseau a traversé l'hiver et maintenant porte ses fruits...

Le lendemain...

Demain, un nouveau jour se lèvera...

Bonne chance pour l'année prochaine...

AAA-ARGH !!

Uun gros oiseau marron que je n'avais jamais vu.

FLAP FLAP FLAP FLAP

KAZUKO AVAIT ÉTÉ MANGÉE PAR UN OISEAU.

Postface / Fin

190

BLOODY KISS by Kazuko Furumiya

© 2006 Kazuko Furumiya
All rights reserved.
First published in Japan in 2006 by HAKUSENSHA, INC., Tokyo
French language translation rights in France arranged with
HAKUSENSHA, INC., Tokyo through Tuttle-Mori Agency Inc., Tokyo

Édition française
Traduction : Fédoua Lamodière
Correction : Thomas Lameth
Lettrage : GB One

© 2010, Éditions Glénat
BP 177 – 38008 Grenoble Cedex.
ISBN : 978-2-7234-7116-9
ISSN : 1253-1928
Dépôt légal : janvier 2010

Imprimé en France en janvier 2010
par Hérissey-CPI – 27 000 Évreux
sur papier provenant de forêts gérées de manière durable

www.glenatmanga.com